Cool Cruise

Written by Christine Peymani

PaRRagon

Bath · New York · Singapore · Hong Kong · Cologne · Delhi · Melbourne

First published by Parragon in 2008
Parragon
Queen Street House
4 Queen Street
Bath BA1 1HE, UK

ISBN 978-1-4075-2047-6

Printed in the UK

"I've got Byron Powell for you," a cheerful voice announced over Jade's mobile phone.

"Um ... okay," Jade replied, amused. Byron was a reality show producer who she and her best friends had got to know when they formed their band the Rock Angelz, and had also worked with him on his reality show, *America Rocks Fashion*. It had been a few months since the girls had heard from Byron, so Jade was eager to hear about his latest scheme.

"Jade, are you there?" Byron shouted into the phone.

"Yep," Jade told him.

"Cloe, Sasha, Yasmin, are you there too?" Byron continued.

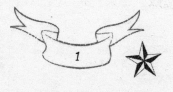

"We're here!" the girls chorused.

"But the question is, where are *you*?" Jade asked, balancing the phone between her ear and shoulder, her hands full of shopping bags as she searched for her car in the mall car park. She heard the sound of whooshing wind and crashing waves, along with laughter and shouts, rushing over the phone line.

"I'm at the beach, of course!" Byron exclaimed. "I'm scoping out ports for my latest show."

"So what can we do for you, Byron?" Sasha inquired. She grabbed her dance bag

©MGA

and dashed out of the studio where she had just finished taking a hip-hop class.

"I need stars for my new show," Byron explained, "and, of course, I immediately thought of you girls!"

"Awesome!" Cloe squealed.

She flourished a paintbrush over her latest canvas, propped on an easel in her room, then set the brush down on her palette so she could focus on the phone call. "But what's the show, anyway?"

"It's a travel show," Byron told the girls, still raising his voice to be heard over the beach noise in the background.

"Travel?" Yasmin chimed in excitedly. She pushed away from her desk, where she'd been writing a short story, and spun around in her chair. "Like, to where?"

"Everywhere, actually," Byron replied.

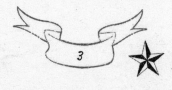
3

"The show will follow you on an around-the-world cruise all summer long."

"That sounds amazing," Jade declared. "When do we start?"

"Well, that's the thing," Byron said. "Shooting starts right away. I'm just here in Fort Lauderdale right now, finalizing the cruise schedule. But if you girls are free, I'll fly you down here tomorrow and we'll get started."

"Tomorrow?" Cloe cried. "But how are we going to pack for an around-the-world cruise in a day?"

"You girls are fashion gurus," Byron replied. "If anyone can do it, you can! Now, can I count on seeing you all here tomorrow?"

"For sure!" the girls chorused.

"All right, then, I'll let you get to your packing," Byron said. "I'm emailing your flight information to you now. See you tomorrow!"

With that, he hung up. Sasha immediately called her three best friends back and conferenced them all together.

"Girls, we have some serious planning to do!" Sasha announced. "I just got the travel plans on my PDA, and we don't leave until tomorrow afternoon, but there's a ton to take care of before then!"

"I'm way ahead of you, Sash," Jade interrupted. She threw her shopping bags into her car, then turned around and headed straight back into the mall. "I'm already at the mall – can you all meet me here?"

"I guess . . . if we have to," Yasmin teased.

"I'll start scoping out swimsuits," Jade told her friends. "Call me when you get here, and we'll start picking out some ship-shape outfits for our big cruise!"

Jade strolled into Beachcomber, a cute new

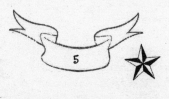

swimwear shop, where she spotted a sweet little pink-and-green-striped bikini. She was searching through the racks for a coordinating sarong when suddenly someone covered her eyes.

"Guess who!" Cloe called.

Jade turned to see her three best friends standing behind her. "Wow, that was fast!"

"Hey, when the mall calls, who are we to drag our feet?" Sasha replied.

"Just let me try on this swimsuit, and then we'll go in search of some nautical gear," Jade told her friends. "Oh, but do you girls need new swimsuits, too?"

"Nah," Yasmin said. "I'm still happy with the lavender tankini I bought last summer."

"And I just picked up a chic little black-and-white number, so I'm all set," Sasha added.

"Cloe?" Jade asked. "You know you can

BRATZ YACHT CLUB · EST. 2001 · SAILOR GIRL

6

never have too many swimsuits, especially on an around-the-world cruise!"

"Normally, I would agree with you," Cloe began, "but I already have five cute suits, so I should probably save my cash for a few other essentials."

"Okay then, I'll be right back," Jade declared.

"Jade, wait!" Yasmin called after her.

"What's up?" Jade asked, stopping short in front of the dressing rooms.

"I think this sarong would be totally adorable with that bikini," Yasmin replied. She held up a hot-pink, ruffled sarong

that perfectly matched the stripes on Jade's halter-neck swimsuit.

"Oh my gosh, that's exactly what I was looking for!" Jade exclaimed. "See, I knew there was a reason we were best friends."

"And that reason is my ability to find stylish sarongs?" Yasmin teased.

"Among other things," Jade joked back. Yasmin handed her the sarong, and Jade hurried into the fitting room. She emerged moments later looking very happy.

"I take it the swimwear was a success?" Sasha asked.

"How could you tell?" Jade wanted to know.

"You just had the look of a satisfied shopper," Sasha replied.

"Well, I hope your shopping quota isn't filled up yet," Cloe interjected, "because we

have a lot more to do!"

"Oh, Cloe, I thought you knew me better than that!" Jade exclaimed. "If there's shopping to be done, I'm totally there!"

Giggling, the girls followed Jade to the checkout, and then back out into the mall.

"Sasha, did that email say where we were going on the cruise?" Yasmin asked.

"No – just that we're flying into Fort Lauderdale, and then back from New York eighty days later," Sasha informed her.

"Eighty days!" Cloe gasped. "That's a big trip!"

"Well, it's a big planet," Jade pointed out. "It's gonna take ages to sail all the way around it, especially since I'm sure Byron's built in time for us to do loads of fun stuff along the way."

"It says in his email that we'll be covering

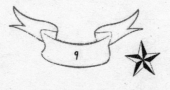

exciting activities in each port for the show," Sasha agreed.

"Omigosh, I forgot we're gonna be on TV!" Cloe cried. "Now I really have to get some cool new clothes for this cruise!"

The girls strutted into Fashion Friend-zy, a shop where they always found fabulous threads.

"Ooh, I'm loving these nautical looks," Sasha declared, checking out a display of outfits all in red, white, blue and black. She picked up a striped, knitted dress and smiled. "Yeah, I think this is camera-ready!"

Cloe grabbed a pair of flared jeans with skinny braces, and a long-sleeved, red-and-white-striped tee. "Perfect for those chilly days on the high sea!" she declared.

Jade held up a pair of sailor shorts with embroidery detail and a red, ruffled top. "I'm

feeling this sailor vibe," she chimed in.

"Totally!" Yasmin agreed, scoping out a blue-and-white dress with gold marine buttons.

"Well, girls, I think we've found the perfect style for our trip," Jade announced. "Luckily, Unique Boutique had a nautical display too, so everything I bought earlier today will fit in with our new look!"

"That's why you're our fashion guru," Cloe declared. "You're always ahead of the game!"

"Girls, we'd better get moving," Sasha pointed out. "We only have a few hours to shop and pack for a three-month trip!"

The girls dashed through the mall, buying anything they could find with nautical stripes or hip marine graphics like anchors, ship wheels and stars. Within the hour, each girl was overloaded with shopping bags.

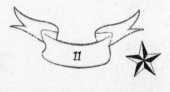

"Now that's what I call a shopping trip!" Jade said, gazing approvingly at her friends' armfuls of bags.

"But now I think I'm gonna need a bigger suitcase!" Cloe wailed, making all of her friends laugh as they headed back to their houses to pack like crazy.

Chapter 2

The next morning, Sasha made her rounds to each of her best friends' houses with a checklist of everything they would need for 80 days at sea. She wore a sailor hat at a jaunty angle over her mahogany-coloured hair to get into the spirit, and pretended she was the ship's captain, preparing her shipmates for an exciting voyage into unknown adventures.

"Well, am I seaworthy?" Jade teased after Sasha finished examining her luggage, checking items off on her list as she went. Cloe and Yasmin stood by with their own suitcases, awaiting Sasha's final approval.

"We all are!" Sasha replied. "I have to say, I am impressed with you girls! You thought of everything – even a few things I forgot, like

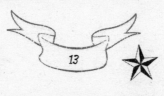

13

aloe vera in case of sunburn and energy bars to ward off between-meal hunger attacks!"

"What?" Yasmin gasped, looking at Jade and Cloe in amazement. "We thought of something the great Sasha didn't? Impossible!"

"It's not that," Sasha protested. "It's just, I tried to be so thorough when I made this list that I can't believe I forgot anything!"

"It's okay," Jade assured Sasha, putting her arm around her friend. "It

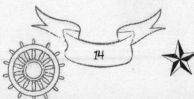

14

happens to the best of us."

"Thanks, Jade," Sasha replied, laughing. "I really do think we're all set. And it's a good thing too, because it's time to head to the airport!"

Jade's parents were waiting to take the girls to the airport. The other girls had said goodbye to their parents at home, but Jade's mum and dad wanted to spend every last moment with their daughter.

The four best friends climbed into Jade's mum's mini-van, their massive amounts of luggage crammed into the back and piled on their laps, filling every spare inch of the van and even blocking the rear windscreen.

"I can't see anything past all your suitcases!" Jade's mum complained.

Jade leaned her head out of the window and declared, "You're clear!" Her mum backed

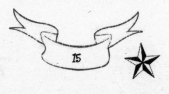
15

timidly out of the driveway, seeming not to believe Jade's assessment.

"I just can't believe my little girl is travelling around the entire world!" Jade's dad exclaimed as the mini-van crawled down the street.

"Dad!" Jade cried, embarrassed.

"Okay, then, I can't believe my very-grown-up daughter is circling the globe," her dad replied. "Is that better?"

"It'll do," Jade agreed. Her dad turned around in his seat so he could see her, and the two shared a smile.

"My mum was freaking out this morning," Cloe told the others. "She kept running around and throwing things she thought I might need on my bed."

"Aww, that's sweet!" Yasmin said, but Cloe shook her head.

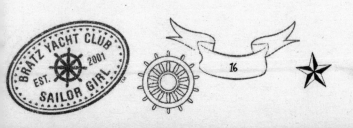

"You don't understand – she literally wanted me to pack everything in the house!" Cloe explained. "She brought me coffee mugs, picture frames, stuffed animals – it was just way too much stuff!"

"Um, Clo, are you sure you didn't pack all of that?" Sasha teased. "Because I've seen your suitcase, and it *looks* big enough to hold everything in your house!"

"Hey!" Cloe protested, giving Sasha a playful shove in the seat beside her.

"You *do* tend to over-pack," Yasmin pointed out.

"I just like to be prepared!" Cloe insisted, but her best friends just laughed.

"Jade, do you think you should have brought a bigger suitcase?" Jade's mum asked worriedly. "I thought you could have used another jacket, and an extra pair of tennis

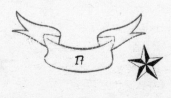

shoes, and maybe some more socks ... do you want to stop and buy some more socks?"

"Mum, believe me, I am all set on clothes," Jade replied.

"Okay ..." her mum said, not sounding like she believed it.

They pulled up at the airport and the girls scrambled out from under their suitcases, dragging their bags out after them. Jade hugged both of her parents, then followed her friends inside, while her mum called after her, "Be careful! Eat your vegetables! And don't forget to write!"

"Parents," Jade complained once they were out of earshot.

"Hey, you should be glad they care!" Sasha told her. "I mean, I'm not completely sure mine were even listening when I told them I was about to sail around the world."

"Your parents care!" Yasmin protested as they joined the end of a winding queue to check in their baggage. "They're just really, really busy, that's all."

"Yeah, I know," Sasha admitted, struggling to pull her piles of bags after her.

"There are always so many relatives crammed into my house, my parents literally might not notice I'm missing from the crowd," Yasmin added.

"Oh, come on, you have the closest-knit family I've ever seen," Cloe pointed out as they inched forward in the queue. "I'm sure they're all lost without you already!"

"Yeah, you're probably right," Yasmin replied with a grin.

Once their bags were checked in, the girls had to wait in a long security queue, and then wait to board their plane.

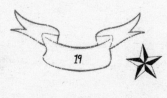

19

"Wow, if you girls weren't here with me, this would be seriously boring!" Jade declared.

"Yeah, flying is a big production," Sasha agreed.

Once they were finally on the plane, Sasha turned on her MP3 player, Yasmin started reading a novel, Jade whipped out a fashion magazine and Cloe pulled out her sketchpad. The girls were so engrossed in their favourite activities that the flight whizzed by, and they were surprised at how soon the pilot announced that they were about to land.

"I can't wait to see Byron again!" Cloe squealed.

"I can't wait to find out exactly where we're going," Sasha chimed in as the girls grabbed their hand luggage and made their way off the plane. "I mean, it isn't like Byron to be so last-minute about everything."

"Maybe the point of the show is that it's a surprise," Cloe suggested excitedly, "and he couldn't tell us anything because it would ruin it! Or maybe another producer was trying to steal it, so he had to keep everything a secret to protect his concept!"

Her friends exchanged amused glances. Cloe tended to get carried away by her ideas, and once she got going, there was no bringing her back down to earth.

"Well, whatever it is, we can ask him right now!" Sasha declared. Just past the security gate, she spotted Byron holding up a big sign reading 'Cloe, Jade, Sasha and Yasmin'.

"There you are!" he exclaimed. "It's been so long since I've seen you that I thought I'd better bring a sign, just to make sure you would recognize me."

"We could never forget you!" Cloe cried.

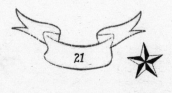

"Especially since we see you on TV every week," Jade pointed out.

"Oh – right – didn't think about that," Byron admitted. "Well, anyway, I'm so glad you girls were available on such short notice! I just pitched this show at the last minute, and the network went for it, so I needed to find people, fast."

"Well, we're glad we're the people you found,' Sasha replied.

"I have quite the adventure in store for you," Byron continued excitedly. "Just let me collect the other teams, and then we'll be off to the dock."

Byron bustled off, while the girls exchanged confused glances. "What does he mean, 'other teams'?" Sasha wondered. "I thought this was supposed to be *our* show!"

Chapter 3

"Girls, I'd like you to meet the competition!" Byron exclaimed. Six boys and two girls trailed behind him, and Byron urged them forward.

"First, the boys' team: Gavin, Trevor, Luke and Noah," Byron began. Each of the boys stepped forward and shook hands all around.

"And our co-ed team: Max, Colin, Reagan and Aubrey," Byron continued.

The two boys and two girls gave the others slight nods in acknowledgment, though they hung back.

"Wait, I don't get it," Cloe protested. "How are all 12 of us going to host a show together?"

"We *aren't*," the tall brunette Byron had

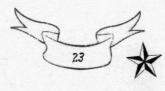

introduced as Reagan snapped. "It's a contest. And once we win, *we'll* be hosting the show."

"Yeah!" her teammates cheered, giving each other high fives.

Byron looked concerned about the team's attitude, but he tried to cover for them, quickly adding, "Er, yes, the winning team will get their very own show. Should be an exciting competition!"

"How are we supposed to do competitive travelling?" Jade wanted to know.

"It's a scavenger hunt," Byron explained. "You'll travel around the world together on a luxurious cruise ship. In each port, you'll receive a clue that will lead you to a cool local spot. I'll provide you with digital cameras with a date-time stamp feature, so you can take a photo at each location to document that you've solved the clue. Whoever gets there first wins the most points. You'll also participate in

exciting local activities at each port, and we'll film your coverage of those. I'll be coming along on the boat with you, as will my fellow producer, Anya, and we'll be awarding points for the team who does the best segment at each port. Make sense?"

The teenagers all stood staring at Byron, trying to process all the information he had just spewed at them. After a moment, he clapped his hands together to snap them out of it.

"All right then!" he said. "I'll take that as a yes. Now, I believe you all have luggage to collect, so I'll just have the limo driver pull around, and I'll meet you outside. Anya is already at the

©MGA

dock, so you'll get to meet her soon."

He gave them all a wave and dashed out of the terminal, leaving the 12 teens staring at each other.

"Well, this should be fun," said the floppy-haired boy who had introduced himself as Noah.

"Yeah, it'll be fun when we win," muttered the gangly redhead, Colin.

Smirking, he and his team strutted off. They returned moments later with their matching, silver designer suitcases while the others were still waiting for their bags, watching battered leather bags and bulging, flowered suitcases circling around and around the conveyor belt.

"Catch you outside!" called Aubrey, the petite girl from the other team. She flipped her long, strawberry blonde hair over her shoulders and stalked out outside, with her teammates following close behind.

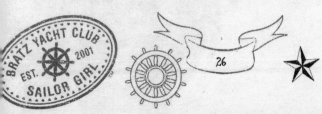

"Huh," Sasha began. "I don't know if 'fun' is exactly the right word."

"Well, *we'll* have fun, anyway," Yasmin pointed out. "I mean, we're going to the coolest spots in the world – how could we not have a spectacular time?"

"It *does* sound really exciting," Jade admitted.

"But I don't want to be cooped up on a boat with the Mean Team out there for three months!" Cloe complained.

"They were pretty awful!" said Trevor, a short guy with curly, black hair.

"You know what, though?" Luke, a spiky-haired blonde began. "If we stick together, we can have an awesome time, and not even worry about those guys."

"I like the way you boys think!" Sasha declared. She spotted her suitcase on the

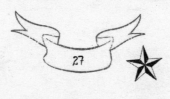

conveyer belt, and soon they had all grabbed their bags and were headed for the kerb.

By the time they reached the limo, they were all talking and laughing like old friends. The Mean Team glared at them as they piled into the back of the car.

"What took you so long?" demanded Max, a muscular guy with a shaved head.

"Apparently the baggage claim didn't get the memo about your very tight schedule," Jade replied, rolling her eyes.

"Whatever," Max muttered. He and the other three members of his team scooted to the far end of the limo and leaned their heads together, whispering and occasionally glancing over at the others, then laughing.

"So how do you guys know Byron?" Yasmin asked, pointedly ignoring the Mean Team.

Byron was sitting in the front beside the

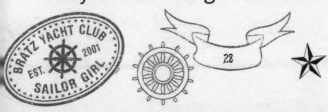

driver, so he didn't see the drama in the back of the car.

"Oh, my dad's a producer too," explained Gavin, the fourth member of the boys' team, sounding embarrassed. "They were working on another show together, and then this one got picked up, and Byron needed teams of high-school kids, so my dad suggested me and my best friends."

"How cool!" Jade declared.

"We're all best friends, too," Cloe added, shooting Gavin a flirtatious smile.

"Well, isn't that special," Reagan sneered, eavesdropping on their conversation.

"Now you look here, you little–" Sasha began fiercely, but Yasmin laid her hand on Sasha's arm, trying to calm her down.

"It *is* pretty special to get to go on a trip like this with all your best friends," Yasmin pointed out. "Are you four best friends, too?"

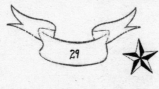

The members of what Cloe had dubbed the Mean Team sniggered. "Um, *no*," Aubrey replied. "This isn't about being good buddies. This is about winning. And we make an awesome team."

"Oh," Jade said. "Well, I guess that's good too. But personally, I'd rather have fun with my friends than win this competition."

"Totally!" her best friends agreed.

"Glad to hear it," Max informed her. "That'll make it all the easier for us to crush you."

"Okay," Sasha replied with a shrug. "Whatever you say."

Sasha loved to win, so it wasn't easy for her to listen to the Mean Team's nasty talk. But she decided that there was no point in arguing, and anyway, she felt sure that she and her best friends would win, no matter what those bad sports said.

Chapter 4

"Here it is — your floating home for the next 80 days!" Byron proclaimed, gesturing dramatically towards the large black-and-white cruise ship waiting in the dock as his teams climbed out of the limo.

"Ooh, it matches my outfit," Sasha pointed out, doing a quick twirl in her black-and-white-striped dress and making her friends laugh.

"Come on now, all aboard!" Byron urged. Several porters met them at the dock and began unloading luggage from the limo, while the 12 teens followed Byron up the gangway, chattering excitedly all the way.

"This will be the boys' deck, and girls, you're upstairs," Byron explained. "Beyond

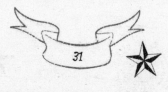

31

that, you can take your pick of rooms. There are 20 suites on this ship, and they're all yours – except for mine at the end there." He pointed to the room at the far end of the hall, and the boys started their search.

Aubrey and Reagan immediately dashed for the stairs, while Cloe, Jade, Sasha and Yasmin followed them at a leisurely pace.

"Ten rooms for six girls seems like decent odds," Jade declared.

"Oh yes, every room on this ship

is utterly luxurious," Byron assured them.

"I like the sound of that!" Yasmin called down from the winding staircase that led to the upper deck.

On the lower deck, Max and Colin were darting from room to room, opening doors and then slamming them shut again, apparently searching for the perfect suite.

"What do you say we just let them figure it out?" Luke suggested to his friends.

"Sure," Noah agreed. "You heard Byron – any of these rooms will be great."

"Ha-ha, you snooze, you lose!" Max taunted them. He and Colin disappeared into rooms at the far end of the hall, across from each other, apparently having decided that those were the best spots on the ship.

With a shrug, the others opened the doors to the rooms nearest them, and were

 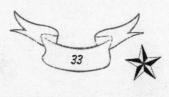 

completely blown away.

"Whoa – all this is for us?" Trevor asked, surveying the spacious suite.

"We've spared no expense on this show!" Byron declared. Then, looking sheepish, he added, "And, of course, the cruise line donated the ship so it could be featured on TV."

"Makes sense to me!" Gavin replied.

Upstairs, the girls were similarly amazed by their rooms. Aubrey and Reagan had locked themselves into their chosen suites, but the other girls all had their doors open, pointing out new discoveries to each other as they explored their rooms.

"I'm loving this Jacuzzi tub!" Cloe announced, scoping out the totally awesome bathroom.

"Mmm, this bed is sooo comfy!" Jade

declared, flopping down in the middle of her king-sized bed.

"Girls, did you see these flat-screen TVs?" Sasha cried, standing in the middle of her own little living room. She turned on the TV and one of her favourite comedies appeared, looking crisp and larger than life. "Nice!"

"Ooh, you have to check out the view!" Jade called, stepping out onto her balcony and enjoying the cool ocean breeze that whipped through her long black hair.

Just then, Reagan poked her head out of her suite.

"Can you girls keep it down?" she asked. "Some of us have better things to do than to listen to your chit-chat."

"Then don't listen!" Sasha retorted. Her best friends all came to their doorways to see what was happening.

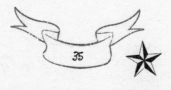

"Humph!" Reagan replied, slamming her door shut again.

"Oh, dear, I guess she's not talking to us anymore," Jade said, joining her friends in the hallway.

"You guys, we have to be on this ship together for the next three months – maybe we should try to make friends with them," Yasmin suggested, looking worried. She couldn't stand to see people bickering like this.

"They haven't said one nice thing since we met them!" Sasha protested.

"Yeah, but that doesn't mean we should stoop to their level," Yasmin pointed out.

"That's true," Cloe had to agree. "Hey, what if we were just super-sweet to them? It might make it harder for them to be so mean to us."

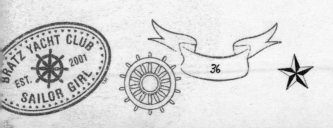

"Couldn't hurt," Jade replied.

"Girls!" Byron called from downstairs. "Let me give you the grand tour, and then you're off to Grand Cayman!"

"Oh wow, I've always wanted to visit a Caribbean island!" Yasmin squealed. "Did you know it's, like, 75 degrees and sunny every day on Grand Cayman?"

"That sounds amazing!" Cloe cried as they hurried down the stairs.

"First, here's the cyber lounge," Byron began, leading them all into a lobby area just past the cabins, which was stocked with rows of flat-panel computers in front of comfy-looking chairs. "You can check email from

©MGA

anywhere in the world right here!"

"That's a relief!" Cloe exclaimed. "I didn't know *how* I was going to survive without email for three months!"

"And here's the restaurant where you'll have dinner every night you're aboard the ship," Byron continued. "But don't worry – we've got an amazing chef who will keep your meals exciting."

"We certainly have," agreed a sophisticated-looking woman in a linen trouser suit, striding up to them. Her golden hair was tucked neatly into a bun, and a pair of thin, wire-rimmed glasses were perched on her nose.

"Hello, everyone, I'm Anya," she added. As each of the teenagers introduced themselves, she repeated their names back in a soft voice, clearly trying to memorize them all. "I do hope you saved me a room."

"We left the best one for you, Anya," Aubrey gushed. "The suite at the far end of the hall, just like the one Byron has."

"Why thank you," Anya replied with a smile. "Aubrey, is it?" When the girl nodded, Anya continued, "That was very thoughtful of you."

Sasha exchanged annoyed looks with her friends, but she knew they couldn't say anything without sounding snotty.

"Glad you could join us," Byron told his colleague. "Is everything in order?"

"It is," she confirmed. "I was just getting the crew all set up on the lower deck."

"Well, now that we're all here, why don't we get on with the tour?" Byron suggested.

He pointed out the café where they could have breakfast, lunch and snacks, then took them upstairs to check out the gym and spa.

 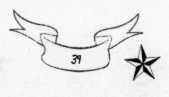 

"There are daily yoga and pilates classes up here," Byron told them, "and you're welcome to get massages and facials here in the spa."

"Oh yeah, I could get used to this!" Sasha declared.

Next, he pointed out the screening room, where he said they could watch as many movies as they liked. The girls were all movie buffs, so they thought that was very good news.

Then he showed them the library, and Yasmin ran in, eagerly checking out the collection of books.

"Didn't you pack, like, ten books?" Jade asked her.

"Yeah, but that's not enough to last me 80 days!" Yasmin replied. "I just didn't have room for more. I'm so relieved there's a library – I

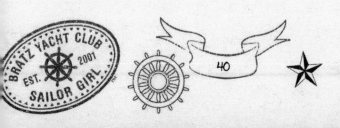

was sure I was going to run out of books!"

"Well, we can't have that, can we?" Sasha teased.

Yasmin was constantly reading, sometimes even several books at once, so her friends knew she wasn't kidding about needing this many books to choose from.

"Oh cool, there are board games in here too," Luke pointed out. "That would be a fun way to spend a long day at sea."

"Um, that would be a *lame* way to spend a day *anywhere*," Reagan muttered, softly enough that the adults wouldn't hear, but loud enough that the other teams would.

"Luke, I love board games," Jade declared. "Anytime you want a little competition, you're on!" He shot her a grateful look as they all followed Byron and Anya to the ship's top deck.

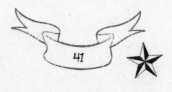

"And this, of course, is the swimming pool," Byron said.

"Ooh, I know where I'll be spending my days!" Cloe squealed, admiring the tranquil turquoise water.

"There's also an observation lounge over there," Anya added, pointing to the other end of the deck. "It has these incredibly comfortable wicker chaise longues with panoramic views of the ocean."

"Can I get one of those at my house?" Jade joked, but her smile faded when she caught Reagan and Aubrey rolling their eyes.

"So, that's the ship," Byron announced, oblivious to the tension between the teams. "Now, who's hungry?"

"I am!" chorused everyone but the Mean Team, who trailed sullenly behind the others as they all made their way back down to the restaurant.

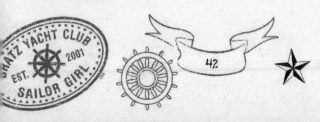

After dinner, Cloe, Jade, Sasha and Yasmin gathered in Yasmin's room to discuss the Mean Team.

"They're going to ruin the whole trip!" Cloe wailed. Dinner had been delicious, but the constant sniping from Max, Colin, Reagan and Aubrey had made it hard to focus on the tasty treats.

"Only if we let them," Sasha declared. "And we are *not* going to let them ruin such an amazing adventure, now are we?"

"No way!" her best friends exclaimed.

"Okay then," Sasha replied with a firm nod. "Let's get out there and win this thing!"

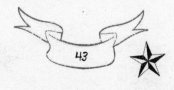

43

The girls spent the next day sunbathing, swimming and researching Grand Cayman so they would have an edge in working out their clue when they reached the island.

Early the following morning, they stepped onto the white, sandy beaches of Grand Cayman for the first time.

"This really is paradise," Yasmin sighed.

"All right, teams, here are your clues," Anya announced, handing each team a sealed blue envelope.

"And here are your digital cameras," Byron added, passing out cute little cameras to the three teams. "They're waterproof, so you can take them anywhere. Just don't forget to

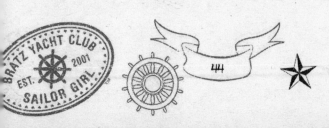

44

document your finds!"

"Also, I've booked activities for each of you," Anya continued. "Girls, you'll be snorkelling with the stingrays."

"How cool!" Cloe squealed.

"Guys, you'll be scuba diving at a shipwreck just off the coast," Anya continued.

"That sounds awesome," Gavin declared.

"And I've got our co-ed team scheduled for ocean kayaking along the coast," Anya finished.

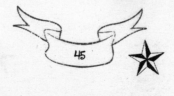

"That's not fair!" Aubrey complained. "They got way better activities than we did."

"Oh, I assure you, ocean kayaking is an amazing experience," Byron said brightly. "Now go on – you've all got a big day ahead of you!"

The teams all headed in opposite directions, and once they were out of earshot of the others, Sasha opened their envelope and read the clue aloud: "Everything's peachy keen under the sea!"

The girls looked thoughtful for a moment, and then Yasmin gasped, "I've got it! 'Peach' like the colour, which is close to coral, and 'keen' could mean sharp, like the jagged edges of a reef. Some of the best coral reefs in the world are off the eastern coast of the island – that's got to be it!"

"You're a genius, Yas!" Jade declared.

They grabbed a cab and rode to the other side of the island, where they rented snorkelling equipment and snapped some underwater photos as they swam alongside the reef.

"We definitely got here first," Sasha announced proudly.

"Now let's go and meet those giant stingrays!" Cloe added.

The girls headed back to Stingray City, where they were amazed at the huge, silvery rays drifting along on top of the water.

"How can we snorkel here?" Jade wondered. "I don't see any space in between the stingrays!"

But they pulled on their snorkelling masks and fins anyway, and followed their guide, Carlson, into the warm, clear water.

"Would you like to hold a ray?" Carlson

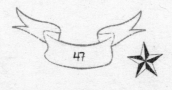

asked, and before the girls could respond, he had gently placed a stingray that was bigger than Yasmin into her outstretched arms.

"Ooh, it's velvety!" she declared, surprised that the creature wasn't slimy at all.

Jade took a picture of Yasmin with the ray, and then each of them took a turn holding it, with the guide's help.

Carlson led them further out so they could swim with the stingrays, and the girls dipped underwater, breathing through their snorkels, and marvelling at the rays floating past them as brightly coloured tropical fish flitted all around.

"Snorkelling at Stingray City offers a window into a magical undersea world that is breathtakingly beautiful and full of surprises," Sasha announced for the camera. Her friends had to smile at her polished presentation, even

in the midst of such a stunning experience as this.

After over an hour in the water, Carlson told them it was time to head back to their boat.

"Who needs to go around the world?" Jade asked. "I think I'll just stay here!"

"I *told* you Grand Cayman was perfect," Yasmin declared.

"We Caymanians like to think so," Carlson agreed. He led them back to their cruise ship, and as it pulled away from the dock with all of its passengers on board, he waved until they were out of sight.

"Okay, we *have* to go back there for a nice, long trip sometime," Sasha announced.

"Spring break, anyone?" Cloe suggested, and her friends readily agreed.

"How was everyone's first day of

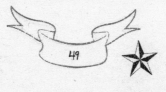

exploration?" Byron asked once they had all gathered in the lounge.

"Spectacular!" Cloe exclaimed.

"Well, let's see how spectacular," Byron continued. "Can I see everyone's scavenger hunt photos?"

He took each team's cameras and examined the pictures they'd taken. "It appears that the girls' team is the clear winner."

"What?" Max shouted. "No way they got there before us!"

"The date-time stamp doesn't lie," Sasha informed him.

"You girls totally cheated!" Reagan protested.

"Now, now, there's no need for that," Byron said calmly. "We're all friends here."

The girls' and guys' teams exchanged

glances at that, but kept quiet.

"We're looking forward to watching your tapes tonight," Anya added. "We'll let you know which segment we liked the best tomorrow."

The girls were exhausted but happy when they headed for their beds that night, and they couldn't wait to move on to their next adventure!

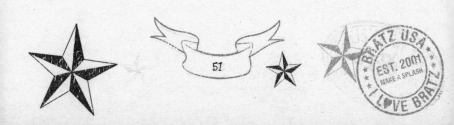

Chapter 6

"It wasn't an easy decision, but the segment we chose this round was submitted by the boys' team," Anya announced over omelettes and French toast the next morning.

"Congratulations!" Yasmin exclaimed, as the Mean Team sulked. "Can we see their footage?"

"Of course," Anya agreed. After breakfast, they all filed upstairs and settled into plush velvet seats in the screening room.

The boys appeared on-screen, decked out in wetsuits and scuba masks. The camera showed them diving and swimming among the ruins of an old ship, following fish that darted past.

"Many tropical fish are drawn to the wreckage, and have made their homes here, slowly claiming this ship for their underwater world," Gavin's voice said over the images.

"The wreckage also attracts divers like us," Noah's voice chimed in, "as it offers an intriguing setting to explore, with a unique combination of reef and wreckage unlike any other in the ocean."

After a few more shots of the boys scuba diving in and around the shipwreck, the reel stopped, and the girls applauded loudly while the Mean Team sat silent, their arms crossed over their chests.

"That was amazing, you guys!" Cloe gushed.

"I love how you worked in the narration," Sasha added. "We'll have to try more of that – hope you don't mind!"

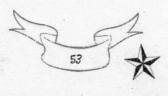

"Not at all," Trevor assured her. "We're all in this together, right?"

"These people don't seem to understand the meaning of 'competition'," Colin hissed to his teammates, but everyone else was too busy talking about the clip to listen to him.

After another day on the ocean, they arrived in Costa Rica. By then, the teams were all eager to disembark and feel solid land beneath their feet again.

Anya passed out the clues, and Byron

©MGA

announced their activities for the day. "Girls, you'll be taking a horseback ride through the rainforest. Boys, you'll kayak through the jungle. And our third team will canoe down the river."

"Ugh, I am so sick of boats," Aubrey muttered. "Cruise ships, kayaks, canoes – it's like, enough already!"

But the others were too engrossed in solving their clues to pay any attention to her.

"It's a fruit, not a tree, and it's very prickly!" Jade read. "Ooh, I've got it – it's got to be the pineapple plantation that's in the middle of the rainforest."

"Good thinking, Jade!" Sasha exclaimed. "Let's go!"

Their guide, Natalia, drove them to the farm, where the girls took pictures with their arms full of freshly picked pineapples. As they

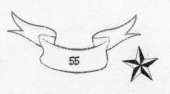

were leaving for their horseback ride, they spotted the boys on their way in.

"Oh man, you beat us again!" Noah cried.

"Looks like you still beat the Mean Team, though," Yasmin assured him. "And anyway, you guys are ahead on the part that really counts – making good TV!"

"I'm sure you girls will give us a run for our money there," Noah told her, smiling.

As their Jeep pulled away, Yasmin couldn't help glancing over her shoulder to catch another glimpse of Noah before the jungle leaves obscured her view.

Next, Natalia took the girls to the ranch where their trail ride would start. Each girl was assigned a horse and climbed into the saddle.

"There is no better way to drink in the wild beauty of the rainforest than from on horseback," Yasmin told the cameras.

"Check out the frogs!" Jade gasped, and the camera zoomed in on several bright red frogs with blue legs. "There's amazing wildlife all around us here – in all sorts of spectacular colours!"

"The views from this trail are utterly breathtaking," Cloe chimed in. They were all making a much bigger effort to contribute to the narration, now that they had seen what a difference it had made in the boys' footage.

After two hours of winding through the jungle trails on horseback, the girls returned to the stable.

"Can I keep her?" Yasmin asked, hugging her golden horse's neck.

"I don't think she'll fit on the boat," Jade teased her, gently pulling her friend away from the horse. Yasmin was a true animal lover, and she always wanted to take every animal she met home.

 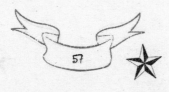 

"Thank you, Goldie," Yasmin said, patting her mare's neck in farewell. "I'll never forget our jungle trek!"

Back at the boat, Byron checked their cameras again.

"I'm sorry girls, I think you misunderstood the clue," he announced, shaking his head. "You were supposed to go to the Sloth Sanctuary, not the Pineapple Farm."

"But that's where the clue led us!" Jade protested.

"Us too," Luke chimed in. They handed their clues to Byron, and he stared at them, puzzled.

"Anya, you didn't switch the clues, did you?" he asked.

"No," she replied. "So someone else must have." Turning to the Mean Team, she enquired, "May I see your clue?"

Reagan reluctantly handed it over, and Anya announced, "Well, they got the right clue. That certainly is strange."

"Hmm." Byron stared at each camera image for a moment, then declared, "Since there seems to have been some sort of mix-up, I'm still going to award the points to the team that got to their clue's answer first. Once more, the speed award goes to our girls."

"That's not fair!" Aubrey complained. "How can they win when they went to the wrong place?"

"Their goal was further away than yours, and they still beat you there," Byron replied. "What isn't fair is that someone switched the clues on them!"

"That doesn't seem right, does it?" Sasha asked, narrowing her eyes at the Mean Team, but they didn't reply.

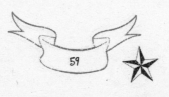

At breakfast the next morning, Byron announced that the girls' team's segment for the previous day had been the best one.

"We could win too if we didn't keep getting stupid activities," Max grumbled.

"Maybe it's just me, but I have trouble thinking of anything that wouldn't be awesome to try in the amazing places we're visiting," Jade pointed out.

After they finished eating, they all watched the girls' clip in the screening room, and the boys' team members all rushed to congratulate them.

"We really did pick up some tips from you," Sasha admitted.

"Nah, that's pure talent," Trevor assured her, and Sasha thought that she wouldn't mind having the next few days at sea to get to know him a little better.

Chapter 7

While the Mean Team hid out in their own rooms or holed up in the café for hours on end, and Byron and Anya kept busy with planning the logistics of their show, the others took advantage of the fun activities their ship had to offer.

The girls went to yoga classes every day while they were at sea.

"I'm gonna be so fit when this cruise is over!" Yasmin announced.

"Like you aren't already!" Jade teased. Yasmin was a yoga expert – in fact, her friends thought she could have been teaching their yoga class herself!

After class, they met the boys at the pool,

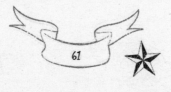

where they swam and splashed around until they were tired, then settled onto lounge chairs, where they all talked until they felt like jumping into the pool again.

Everyone met up for dinner, and then the two teams went up to the library to play board games for a few hours. They would step out on the top deck to see the stars before they went to bed, and in the morning, they would do it all over again.

Although their days on the ocean were very relaxing, after a few had passed by in exactly the same way, everyone on board was starting to go stir crazy.

"Isn't there *anywhere* we can land?" Cloe wondered.

"We're heading for Tahiti," Yasmin explained. "It's one of the most isolated land masses in the world, which is why it takes a while to get to."

"It had better be pretty incredible," Cloe grumbled, but her friends assured her it would be.

"I wonder what the other team's up to," Jade mused. Although they had been spending every day with the boys' team, they had hardly seen the third team since they had left Costa Rica.

"Nothing good, I'm sure," Sasha said, and the others had to agree.

When they finally landed on Tahiti, everyone dashed off the ship in their eagerness to return to dry land.

"I never thought I'd be so happy to see the ground," Jade declared.

"Yeah, the ocean is gorgeous, but it does all start to look the same

after a while," Luke agreed.

"We have an announcement," Anya called, waving her hands to get everyone's attention. "To avoid last time's mishap, we will be reading today's clue aloud, and then we'll give you hard copies so you can continue pondering."

She pulled a neatly folded piece of paper out of her pocket and read, "I am dark but my neighbours are pale."

Sasha's face lit up, and she pulled her friends aside so she could give her answer without anyone else hearing. "It has to be the black sand beach, Point Venus!" she announced. "The beaches around it have white sand, so it totally fits!"

Her friends agreed that she had to be right, and their new guide for the day, Ari, drove them to the beach, where they took cute shots of each other lounging on the sand.

"Now let's check out those Tahitian lagoons," Jade urged.

Their activity for the day was a coastal tour of the island, with stops for snorkelling along the way.

"You know, I'm really loving snorkelling," Cloe declared as she tugged on her fins at their first stop. "It's such an amazing way to see what's going on under the sea."

The girls were having so much fun that it was easy for them to tape an interesting segment. Their guide had to tell them several times that they needed to leave, because they were so entranced by the tropical fish weaving through the reefs beneath them that they didn't want to go. Besides, they were enjoying the chance to be away from the ship after being confined to it for so long.

"Everyone else needs to step up their game," Byron declared when he checked out

 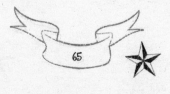 

the day's photos yet again. "The girls have won once more. They're tearing up these clues!"

"They're smart girls – how can we compete?" Trevor asked, as he and his friends gave the girls congratulatory hugs.

"Whatever," Max muttered, glaring at the other teams.

But the next morning, the Mean Team cheered up when their piece on a four-wheel-drive tour of Tahiti's interior, complete with spectacular views and a dip beneath a waterfall, won for the day.

"I knew we could win if we just got something cool to do!" Reagan declared.

The other teams exchanged exasperated looks, but they knew by now that it wasn't worth saying anything to the Mean Team.

As they headed out to sea again, the girls

were happy to find themselves becoming better and better friends with the boys' team.

"Gavin's cute, don't you think?" Cloe asked her best friends in her suite that night.

"I guess," Sasha agreed, "but Trevor's cuter!"

"No way – Noah's the cutest!" Yasmin protested.

"They're all cute, but Luke is adorable *and* funny," Jade interjected, and soon all the girls were listing other good traits for their crushes – Trevor was smart, Gavin was hard-working and Noah was so sweet.

Finally, Sasha declared, "Okay, okay, all our crushes are wonderful guys. Can we all agree on that?"

"For sure!" her friends replied.

"We're just lucky all the teams weren't like the Mean Team," Yasmin pointed out.

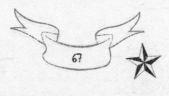

"I don't think *anyone's* as mean as they are," Cloe replied.

"I just don't get it," Jade added from her spot sprawled across Cloe's couch. "*Why* would they want to be so awful?"

"Yeah, and why would they cheat? They had to know they'd get caught," Sasha chimed in.

"Who knows?" Yasmin sighed. "I guess they're just super-competitive and determined to win at all costs."

"Yeah, but they're in last place!" Cloe reminded them.

"Well, that's what makes this trip so much fun," Yasmin said, making her friends giggle. They were rooting for the boys to do well, but since the Mean Team had been so rude from the moment they had met, the girls just couldn't bring themselves to root for them.

Chapter 8

The girls and guys resumed their shipboard routine, hanging out all day long, with some research time thrown in on their next destination, Melbourne, Australia. Because this leg of the journey was another long one, and they had already played all of the board games repeatedly, they started watching movies together in the evenings instead. Byron and Anya usually joined them, and sometimes even the Mean Team came too. They were always invited, just to be polite, and the girls thought they came because at least during a movie, they didn't have to talk to anyone, something they apparently didn't like very much.

"Being in the middle of the ocean *has*

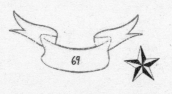

BRATZ USA
★ EST. 2001 ★
MAKE A SPLASH
I LOVE BRATZ

been a great way to catch up on my movie-watching," Jade pointed out.

"I've totally caught up on my reading, too," Yasmin added. Her friends just laughed and shook their heads, so that she had to ask, "What? What's so funny?"

"Yas, you'll *never* have caught up on your reading," Sasha explained, "because you want to read every book in the world!"

"Well, that's true..." Yasmin admitted. "But at least I've made a dent in that list on this trip!"

©MGA

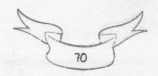

"And we're very proud of you for that," Jade assured her, slinging her arm around her friend's shoulders.

"Oh good," Yasmin replied with a grin.

Although they were keeping busy and building stronger friendships with the boys, it was always more exciting to have a brand-new destination to explore. So when they reached Australia at last, the girls couldn't wait to discover what their next adventure would be.

"You girls will be swimming with the dolphins," Anya informed them once they had disembarked.

"Omigosh, I've always wanted to try that!" Cloe squealed.

Cloe said that about a lot of things, but this time, her friends were right there with her – they couldn't wait to swim with those beautiful, graceful creatures, either!

The boys were going snorkelling with the sea dragons, which sounded amazing too, and the third team would be exploring the outback, encountering kangaroos and koalas in the wild. This time, even the Mean Team couldn't complain – all of their excursions were fantastic!

"I'm liking Australia," Cloe announced, and even though they hadn't seen any of it yet, her friends had to agree. They just had a good feeling about this place.

"And here's your clue," Byron told them. "I'm Australia's bear but I'm no bear."

"Too easy!" Cloe cried, once she and her friends had met up with their new guide, Liz. "Everyone knows koala bears aren't really bears!"

"Good job, Clo!" Sasha exclaimed. "I guess this means we'll get to see some wild koalas after all!"

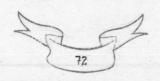

Liz drove them into the outback and helped them spot several fuzzy grey koalas dozing among the branches of their eucalyptus trees. They even got Liz to take a picture of all four of them together, with the koalas in the background.

"That's definitely going in a frame," Yasmin declared when she saw the image on the screen. "We all look fabulous!"

"But Yas, if you framed every photo we looked fabulous in, that would be *way* too many frames!" Jade joked.

"That's true," Yasmin agreed, "but this is the only picture I have where we're looking fabulous with koalas."

Jade had to admit that the koala angle did make this picture stand out from the others they had taken together over the years.

"Koalas, check," Sasha said. "Dolphins, here we come!"

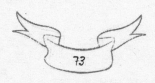

The girls rode a boat out to a popular dolphin habitat, where they donned snorkelling gear and slipped into the water with dolphins leaping and frolicking all around them.

"This is the most amazing experience of my life!" Cloe squealed, and although that was the sort of thing she said a lot, this time her best friends knew it was true.

"The dolphins are so friendly, and they seem so happy to have us here to play with them!" Jade added, looking at the camera on the speedboat alongside her.

"They're totally accepting of us," Yasmin chimed in, trying to explain the experience to the viewers she knew would be watching this segment at home. "They're wild bottlenose dolphins who can't have seen many people, but they're so trusting and willing to let us join in their fun. If only more humans

were this open-minded!"

They spent two hours swimming with the dolphins, and the excitement of it never wore off. Finally, Liz practically dragged them out of the water, pointing out that the ship would be forced to leave without them if they didn't get back soon.

The girls were still jabbering about the dolphins when they rejoined the others, and they were so elated that they didn't even mind that the Mean Team had beat them to tracking down a koala. They knew it was inevitable that eventually someone else would get a scavenger hunt point. They just wished that it had been the boys,

©MGA

who were now lagging behind.

The next day, Byron and Anya announced that the girls' segment was their latest pick.

"I knew our enthusiasm would totally come through on the film," Cloe cried.

"That was definitely the best piece we've done yet," Yasmin agreed.

"Everyone who sees it will want to swim with the dolphins!" Jade declared.

The girls were certain that the Mean Team members were sulking because they had got kangaroos and koalas instead of dolphins, but they were still too pumped up about their latest adventure to listen to that team's complaints.

Besides, the boys had learned from Byron about the girls' singing career, and had begged them to give a concert on the ship.

"We promise we'll be the best audience

you've ever had!" Noah swore.

"We could invite the ship's crew and the TV crew," Gavin added. "It would be a great bonding experience!"

The girls were flattered that their new friends were so interested in their music, so they felt that they couldn't refuse. The next few days at sea passed in a flurry of activity as they ran rehearsals for their show. They had finished a tour just before the cruise began, so they had plenty of material to draw from, but they hadn't sung a note except in the shower for weeks, so they definitely needed to practise.

The night before the ship was docking in Bali, the girls gave a concert on the upper deck, with the stars shining down on them and the ocean glistening all around. Everyone on board the ship, from the captain to the chef, the yoga instructor to the cameraman, gathered to

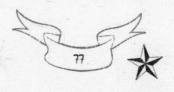

see the show, and the girls gave an incredible performance. They even spotted the Mean Team lurking at the back of the crowd.

Their audience cheered them on, eager for more, but just as the girls were about to launch into an encore, the electricity cut out, leaving them un-miked and cloaked in darkness.

"That's okay," Sasha announced. "This just makes it a more intimate concert." She was sure that the Mean Team had cut the electricity to try to stop the show, and she just wasn't going to let that happen. So the girls sang their final song of the evening a capella, and it was stunningly beautiful, each note hanging in the chilly sea air and seeming to float on forever through the night sky.

The crowd cheered until they were hoarse and clapped until their hands stung. "Well, girls, I think you've found the perfect way to end all your shows," Byron told them.

"If only we could take every crowd out in the middle of the ocean!" Jade teased, and Byron had to admit that that might be a bit of a challenge.

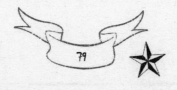

While Australia had been all about adventure, Bali was utterly peaceful. Instead of the challenging outdoor activities they had done during their previous stops, the three teams would be focusing on cultural activities and drinking in the scenery on this tranquil island.

When they left the ship the morning after their concert, as usual they received their assignments for the day. But this time, when Anya read out where each team would be going from her neatly typed sheet, she looked confused.

"Ancient ruins for the girls, fire dance for the boys and safari for our co-ed team," she announced. She peered at the sheet intently,

as though she expected the words to rearrange themselves. "Wait – I thought it was ruins for the boys, safari for the girls and fire dance for the third team. But then it says right here ..." She trailed off, staring at the sheet in sheer puzzlement.

"I don't see why it matters," Aubrey asserted. "After all, it's all about how we cover whatever we're assigned – so the assignments should be totally interchangeable."

"That's true," Anya admitted, though she still seemed uncertain.

"We're fine with it," Sasha declared, though she was sure this was another attempt at sabotage by the Mean Team.

"Us too," Trevor quickly agreed, exchanging a nod with Sasha. They understood each other – if this was how the Mean Team wanted to play it, as their look had said, then the other two teams would just

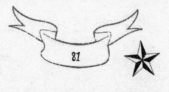

have to beat them anyway, no matter what they tried.

"Well, I guess that's settled then!" Byron said swiftly. He disliked any sort of delay or confusion, so he was eager to have everything back on track again. "Now, today's clue: If you're game for some music, ours can't be beat."

For the first time, the girls had no idea what the clue could mean. They knew they had to come up

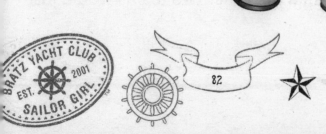

©MGA

with something, so they took a picture with the first Balinese musicians they could find – a group of chanters who were practising for the fire dance the boys would be attending.

"That could be what it meant," Jade said, but her best friends could tell that even she didn't believe that.

Disappointed in their clue-solving abilities for the day, but determined to make up for it with their reporting, the girls followed their latest guide, Kemala, to the streets of the oldest settlement on Bali. From there, they explored the gorgeous Water Palace, built much more recently but still utterly dazzling, and then they hiked through a mountain pass for a view of the entire island.

They enjoyed the change of pace from the previous days' activities, and all four girls felt that they had got some good material, but they knew it couldn't even begin to compare to their dolphin segment.

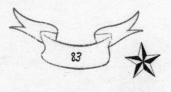

When they girls returned to the boat that day, they were feeling a little down. Bali was beautiful, but it didn't seem to have been very lucky for them. Sure enough, when the clue was revealed, the answer was something they had never even heard of: 'gamelan'.

"This point goes to the boys' team!" Byron declared. The boys burst out in cheers, thrilled to have finally earned a scavenger-hunt point.

"What is that, anyway?" Cloe asked Gavin.

"It's a traditional Balinese percussion group," Gavin explained. "So 'game' is in the word of course, and then 'beat' in the clue refers to drumbeats."

"You are just too clever!" Cloe cooed, making her new crush blush.

"You guys are the ones who have got every other clue right," he pointed out.

"Um, except for the one *we* got," Reagan objected.

"But they still solved that one," Gavin insisted.

"Yeah, well, we *solved* all of them except today's, too," Reagan snapped. "So I don't really see what that proves."

Poor Gavin didn't know what else to say, so Sasha jumped in to defend her new friend. "You know, everything doesn't have to be an argument," she pointed out. "You could just let some things go."

With that, she turned on her heel and stalked back onto the boat, with her friends hurrying after her.

"Geez, what's her problem?" she heard Reagan ask behind her.

"Who knows?" Colin replied. "She's probably just cross that they lost."

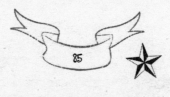
85

"Argh!" Sasha cried. "I just don't think I can take those four much longer!"

"The trip's more than halfway over," Trevor pointed out.

"Yeah, but I don't want the *trip* to end," Sasha told him. "I just wish they weren't on it with us!"

"I know how you feel," he agreed, "but you can't let people like that get to you. You just have to stay chilled."

Jade laughed. "Sasha is not the world's most chilled-out person."

"It's true," Sasha admitted with a shrug. Turning to her three best friends, she added, "But that's why you love me, right?"

"Totally!" they all replied.

The four girls stopped walking in the middle of the hallway to share a group hug before heading back to their rooms.

The following day, the boys were declared the winners of the latest segment contest.

"What?" Max shouted. "But *we* had the coolest thing to cover!"

"We keep telling you it's the reporting, not the topic," Luke pointed out with a shrug. "Maybe now you'll believe us."

"Anyway, what makes you so sure yours was the best activity?" Jade asked. "If I didn't know better, I'd think you had arranged for you guys to get that activity."

"What are you trying to say?" Max demanded.

"Oh, I think you know," Jade replied. She picked up her empty breakfast plate and walked away from the table. Moments later, all of her friends followed, and finally the Mean Team shuffled out of the café as well.

"Okay, what's going on here?" Byron asked.

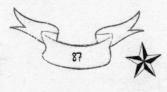

"There seems to be some tension between the teams," Anya told him. "I think we should probably meet with all the contestants today and try to smooth things over."

"You're absolutely right," Byron agreed. He paused, then added, "But how, exactly, will we do that?"

"Don't worry," Anya assured him. "I'm very good at this sort of thing."

They gathered all of their contestants together before lunch, and Anya asked each of them to voice anything that was bothering them. Sasha volunteered to begin, and immediately said, "It bothers me that the co-ed team is trying to cheat."

"We are not!" Colin shouted, leaping out of his chair. His teammates looked like they wanted to do the same, but they appeared to

be restraining themselves.

"That's a very serious accusation," Anya told Sasha.

"I know," Sasha replied. "And I wouldn't say something like that lightly."

"That's true," Byron chimed in. "Sasha always thinks things through very carefully."

"All right, then, what makes you think they've been cheating?" Anya inquired.

"When the clues got switched, they were the only ones who got the right one," Sasha began.

"Don't you think we're smart enough not to point the finger so obviously at ourselves?" Aubrey demanded.

"I think you were desperate to get ahead at any cost," Sasha replied. "And sometimes

 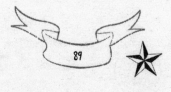 

desperation makes people do silly things."

"Okay, is there anything else?" Anya wanted to know.

"Yeah," Jade chimed in. "They switched the event assignments for yesterday."

"And why would you think that?" Anya asked.

"Remember, you thought they were wrong, too," Jade pointed out. "And they seemed very pleased. Then, when they still didn't win, they were really upset."

"We like to win!" Max protested. "I don't see how that's a crime!"

"I like winning too, but wouldn't you rather win fair and square instead of by cheating?" Yasmin replied.

"We didn't cheat!" Aubrey yelled.

"All right, let's all calm down," Anya

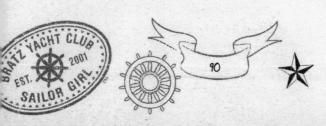

insisted. "Now, is that it?"

"No," Cloe declared. "They also tried to ruin our concert."

"That's not even part of the contest!" Reagan cried. "I don't see what that has to do with anything!"

"It's just another example of lack of respect for the other people on this ship," Cloe replied.

"By which you mean *you*," Reagan sneered.

"Look, I don't know who's wrong or right here," Anya interrupted, "but this needs to stop. And if it doesn't, we'll call off this show right now and send you all home."

"We will?" Byron gasped, but then he saw the determined look in his producing partner's eyes, and he nodded resolutely. "That's right, we will."

"Do you think you can all try to get along?" Anya asked.

"Yes," they all murmured, hanging their heads.

"All right then. No more snide comments, no more accusations, no more back-biting, okay?" Anya continued.

"Yes, Anya," the 12 team members agreed.

"Great!" Anya exclaimed, perfectly cheerful again. "Then let's go have some lunch! I hear our chef has made his famous

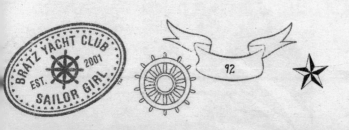

turkey burgers today!"

At Anya's cue, the waiters began bringing out lunch for everyone, but they ate in near silence, wondering how they were going to keep the peace for the next 20 days.

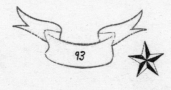

Chapter 10

When they reached Hong Kong, they all spent a day together in the city before separating for various day trips around China. Cloe, Jade, Sasha and Yasmin took a ferry to the island of Macau, a former Portuguese colony that still retained a unique, exotic flavour. But it was when their sightseeing was over that their real Hong Kong adventure began.

The girls needed their passports to return to Hong Kong, but when the girls looked for them, the passports they had carefully hidden in the inside pockets of their coats or bags were all missing.

"Are you sure you brought yours?" Sasha asked her friends, over and over again. "Are

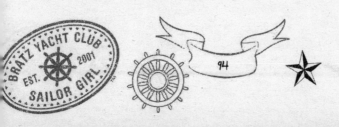

you sure you didn't put it somewhere else?"

But all four were completely gone. Sasha called the cruise ship using the international mobile phone Byron had supplied them with, and Anya promised to meet them at the dock immediately, with the passports in hand.

Sure enough, when she appeared, she was waving four blue passports at them from the deck of the ferry.

"I'm so sorry!" Cloe cried when Anya stepped off the boat. "I don't know how we all managed to forget them, but–"

Anya held up her hand to halt Cloe's apologies. "You didn't forget them."

"Then where were they?" Cloe asked.

"They were with Reagan," Anya said softly.

"Wait, how did you find out?" Sasha wanted to know.

"I'd been thinking about the weird things

 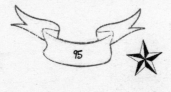 

you'd noticed from that team," Anya began, "and I know Byron trusts you girls, so I didn't want to assume you were totally off-base. And actually, it did all seem to fit. So when I got your call, I decided to search Reagan's room. And there were your passports, hidden in her sock drawer."

"Why would she do that?' Yasmin wondered, her brown eyes wide with hurt. "I mean, I know she's not our biggest fan, but we could have been trapped here without our passports!"

"I know, it's totally unacceptable," Anya replied. "We're sending her on the next plane home."

"And what about the rest of the team?" Jade wanted to know.

"They're going with her," Anya told them. "I don't know if all of them were in on it – in

fact I'm pretty sure Aubrey had no idea what was going on – but the way the competition was set up, it just wouldn't have made sense for her to stick it out alone. And she didn't seem to want to, either."

"It's just so sad," Yasmin sighed. "They weren't nice, but I do think they were all really talented."

"Well, the good news is that this kind of drama is exactly what we need for a reality TV show," Anya pointed out. "I wish it hadn't happened, but it sure won't hurt our ratings!"

When the girls returned to the ship, the Mean

Team members were still packing up their things. Aubrey heard her rivals entering the hallway and ran to meet them.

"I just want to tell you that I'm so sorry about everything that happened," she told them. "I know I was mean to you, but I would never have done any of the things that my teammates did. I'm really ashamed to be grouped together with them."

Her face was red and puffy, and her cheeks were streaked with the faded tracks of tears.

"Thanks for telling us," Yasmin said. "It's good to know that you weren't actually out to get us."

"What are you doing out there, Aubrey?" Reagan shouted from down the hall. "Are you still talking to those bratty girls? Come on, I need you to help me pack!"

Aubrey took a step towards Reagan's

98

room as though about to follow her friend's instructions, but then she stopped herself. "Reagan, would you quit it already?" she demanded. "Haven't you caused enough problems with your crazy rivalry?"

She turned back to the other girls and sighed. "She should be out here apologizing too, but that's really not her style."

"Yeah, we kind of gathered that," Jade replied.

"Well, I'd better get out of here," Aubrey told them. "I don't want to keep you guys from getting to your next port on time."

She headed down the hall, but Yasmin called her back. "Aubrey? I'm really sorry about the way things turned out."

"Me too," Aubrey murmured. "Next time, I just need to pick better teammates. Maybe even go with some best friends, like you girls did."

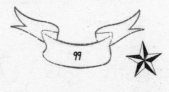
99

No one else from the Mean Team even bothered to say goodbye, but that was fine with the remaining two teams.

There was a much calmer vibe on the cruise ship with the Mean Team gone. The girls finally felt as if they could relax on the boat and just enjoy the fact that they were circling the entire globe.

"So it's just boys against girls now," Sasha pointed out that night at dinner.

"You girls are totally gonna win," Trevor replied.

"I don't know," Jade told him. "We still have a load more cities to go."

"Now that's the sort of friendly competition I like to see," Byron announced, grinning.

"Us too," Yasmin agreed.

Their next stop was Mumbai, from where

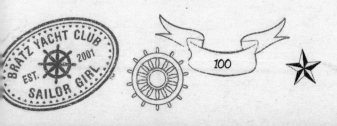

the girls took a trip to the Taj Mahal, while the boys visited the temples on Elephanta Island. Now that they were down to just two teams, Byron and Anya had stopped concocting riddles, and were simply judging each team's ability to communicate to viewers what was truly extraordinary about the place they were visiting.

"This has to be the most beautiful building in the world," Yasmin sighed when she and her best friends stood facing the Taj Mahal.

"Absolutely," Cloe agreed. "You can see so much love in every detail."

"This is what a monument should be," Sasha declared.

Their emotionally charged commentary won their piece first place for the day.

They sailed on to Cairo, where both teams were desperate to see the Pyramids

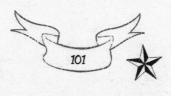

and the Sphinx.

"Please, can't we all go to them together, just this once?" Cloe begged. "It'll be so much more fun that way!"

"We can each discuss different aspects of the monuments," Noah added. "I mean, we'll all be bringing our own perspectives into the mix, so it's not like you're going to get the same piece twice."

"I guess it could work . . ." Anya admitted. Since they were airing the segments filmed throughout this cruise, they had been striving for variety in the previous ports, but Anya and Byron agreed that there was enough to talk about between the Pyramids of Giza and the Sphinx that a single trip would work very well.

That was when the teams came up with the idea to really join forces.

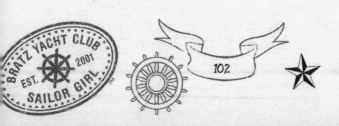

"I think this show would be way better if we were all on it, permanently," Gavin declared.

"Totally!" Cloe agreed instantly. "With so many of us reporting, we could tell people about all sorts of things, instead of just hitting the major sights."

"And we could appeal to all different kinds of travellers, since we each have our own travel style," Jade added.

"I'm in," Sasha chimed in, and the others all nodded their agreement. "Now we just have to convince Byron and Anya!"

When they docked in Cairo, the eight remaining contestants were on a mission. They fanned out to uncover local shopping spots, eateries and lesser-known attractions, plus they covered the region's most famous monuments. They stayed up all night with

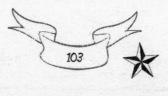
103

the editing team, cutting together a polished episode of a hip, multi-dimensional travel show.

The editors had held Byron and Anya off all night, claiming to be having some problem with their software, so when the producers entered the screening room the next morning, they were expecting to see the usual rough clips that they would choose between.

They watched the completed episode in stunned silence. When it was over, Byron declared, "We could air that tomorrow, just as it is!"

"Fine by us," Sasha told him.

"You know, having eight different reporters worked really well," Anya added. "I thought it would be too many, but it really gave you a range that most travel shows don't have."

"That's what we thought, too!" Cloe exclaimed.

"So is the competition off?" Luke wanted to know. "Can we all be the winners?"

Byron and Anya exchanged questioning looks, then both shrugged and nodded. "I don't see why not," Byron declared, and the teens all cheered.

 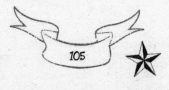

Once the teams had merged, they found themselves having much more fun on their excursions.

"I wish we'd been exploring together the whole time!" Cloe cried. "It's so much more fun this way!"

"And now that it's not a competition, I just feel more natural in front of the camera," Sasha added. "I'm not forcing anything to try to get attention for us."

"Plus now we can really soak up each spot instead of worrying about what the other teams are doing," Noah pointed out.

The eight young people were strolling through the streets of Istanbul as they talked,

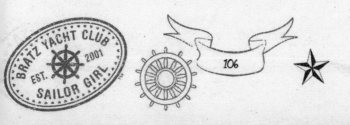

admiring the stunning Blue Mosque and the sprawling Topkapi Palace, the elaborate Church of St Sophia and the winding stalls of the Grand Bazaar.

"I can't believe this is the first chance I've had to shop!" Jade exclaimed, examining a Turkish rug woven in brilliant colours in an intricate pattern. "That alone is proof that this trip has been way too stressful so far."

"I just can't believe we only have five stops left on this cruise," Yasmin pointed out. "When we started, 80 days sounded like forever. But now, it seems like it's gone by so fast."

"Don't you think it'll be weird staying in one place again after travelling this much?" Jade asked.

"We'll still be travelling," Luke reminded her. "I mean, we're starting our very own travel show soon!"

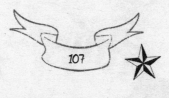

107

"Yeah, but I know what you girls mean," Noah chimed in. "I don't think we'll ever have an adventure quite like this. I mean, around the world in 80 days – that's the chance of a lifetime!"

"Exactly," Yasmin agreed.

"Well, that just means we have to make the most of the rest of the trip," Gavin declared, and they all agreed that they would.

Now that they had reached Europe, their stops became closer together. There were no long stretches of lazy days at sea in between the flurry of activity that came with their arrival in a port. They had been bored by the sailing days at first, but now everyone began to feel nostalgic for them, as they would be soon gone forever.

Their next stop was St Petersburg, Russia, where they scoped out dazzlingly beautiful, delicately carved and brilliantly painted palaces, churches and museums.

From there, they sailed to Santorini, a Greek island known for its quaint, whitewashed villages and sun-drenched beaches. They wandered through the winding village streets, visited ruins and beaches and even saw an active volcano. By then, Byron and Anya were leaving them to explore on their own, rather than planning out every minute of their days as they had for most of the cruise.

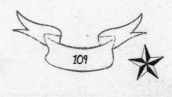

"You'll have to choose your own destinations for your show this year," Byron told them. "So you might as well start finding your own way now."

After so many weeks of extremely structured tours, the girls and guys were all relieved to finally have some time to simply wander. They were still taping segments for the show of course, but the mood had shifted to one of discovery, where they never knew what was around the next corner, and that was the appeal of it all.

Next they went to Venice, where they visited the Doges' Palace and St Mark's Cathedral before splitting into two groups for a gondola ride down the Grand Canal.

"I bet this city looked and felt and sounded exactly like this a hundred years ago," Yasmin sighed.

"Oh, absolutely," Noah agreed. He sat next to her in the gondola and held her hand as they drifted down the canal.

"It really is like stepping into the past," Gavin added.

He and Cloe sat across from their friends, also holding hands as they gazed out at the aging but beautiful buildings they passed.

"I love it!" Cloe shouted, making the others laugh.

©MGA

111

"Well, I do," she continued in a quieter voice.

"Me too," Yasmin told her friend. "There's something magical about it, something impermanent that's totally touching."

Luckily, the camera crew was in a nearby gondola to catch their conversation, which was exactly what they would have wanted to tell other people about this city, but would never have thought of saying if they had forced it to come.

That night, back on board their cruise ship, they all stayed up late, staring at the glowing stars as they glided beneath them.

"I'm so glad we met you guys," Jade declared.

"This cruise wouldn't have been half as much fun without you," Sasha added.

"Aww, you girls are sweet," Trevor replied, giving them a crooked grin. "And our show

next year will definitely be twice as much fun with all of you around!"

They were all still trying to avoid thinking about the cruise coming to an end, and going back to their real lives, with school starting up and chores to be done. They hung out by the pool and played board games like they had for weeks, but always now with the knowledge hanging over their heads that it was almost at an end.

When they reached London, the girls were eager to show their guy friends around, since the boys had never been there before.

"This is where we first met Byron, you know," Jade told the guys. "Back when we first formed the Rock Angelz."

"Wow," Luke teased. "No wonder people say that London's an important historical city."

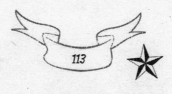

Jade punched him lightly on the arm, but he insisted, "No, no, I'm serious! That's, like, a monumental event!"

They visited all the major attractions: Buckingham Palace, the Tower of London, Westminster Abbey and St Paul's Cathedral. Jade was thrilled to get a bit more shopping in at Covent Garden, a quirky outdoor shopping area she had fallen in love with the last time she was in town.

"Oh no, I still haven't got my mum a souvenir!" Cloe gasped as they wandered through the shops.

"Well then, I'd say this is the perfect time to find something," Sasha said, sensibly.

After much searching, Cloe found a beautiful hand-woven scarf that she just knew her mum would love. "But I've *been* to London before," she complained. "I should've got her

something from somewhere new!"

"You know she'll be thrilled with whatever you give her," Yasmin reminded her friend.

Cloe had to admit that she was right, and bought the scarf.

Before they knew it, Byron and Anya were herding them back onto the boat, and they were heading out to sea, on their way to New York. They would do a final segment for their summer travel show there before flying home at last.

The boys hadn't been to New York before either, so the girls were excited to show them Times Square and the Statue of Liberty,

©MGA

the Empire State Building and Central Park. They all went to a Broadway show together, and of course Jade insisted on a Fifth Avenue shopping excursion.

But then it was time to retrieve their luggage from the ship so that it could start on another tour.

"Goodbye, ship!" Cloe cried as they watched it pull out of port without them for the first time in months. "Thanks for taking us all the way around the world!"

"That really was our home for the past few months," Yasmin added. "I'm really going to miss it!"

"*I'm* going to miss the unlimited spa service," Sasha interjected.

"And the unlimited food!" Jade chimed in.

"I'm gonna miss you girls." Noah said.

"Awww!" the girls all chorused.

"We really will be filming our new show soon," Yasmin reminded him. "So you won't have to miss us for too long."

"The girl has a point," Trevor agreed.

"I can't believe we have our own travel show!" Cloe gasped. "I was so caught up in getting through the cruise that it really hasn't sunk in!"

"Give it time," Sasha told her best friend, smiling. "It will."

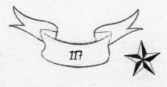

Chapter 12

When classes started the next week, and the girls' English teacher asked them to write about what they had done over their summer holiday, the girls burst out laughing.

"Girls? Do you want to share the joke with the class?" their teacher, Miss Berand, asked, raising her eyebrows at them.

"I just don't think you'd believe us if we told you," Jade explained.

"Okay, now I have to hear it," their teacher replied.

The girls spent the rest of the class detailing their worldwide cruise, and they still hadn't finished when the bell rang,

signalling the end of the school day.

"I guess we'll have to hear more next time," Miss Berand told them as the classroom cleared out.

"Don't you think we should hear from someone else next time?" Yasmin asked.

"Honestly?" Miss Berand replied. "I can't imagine anyone else's summer even beginning to live up to yours. My big summer holiday, for instance, was a weekend trip to Chicago. It's just not the same, you know?"

The girls felt a little embarrassed as they left the classroom. They hadn't wanted to brag about their summer – even though they had to admit it had been a pretty spectacular one. And they certainly hadn't wanted to make anyone else feel bad about how they had spent their holiday.

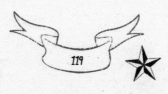
119

"You know it's only going to get worse," Sasha pointed out. "Byron's got us flying around every weekend and on every break to get enough episodes of this show filmed to fill the whole season. So then when people ask what we did over the weekend–"

"We'll have to say, 'I went to Paris' or 'Jamaica' or 'Kyoto'," Yasmin finished for her. "Yeah, you're right, it'll just keep going."

"But you know, there are worse things than having tons of cool trips to talk about," Jade reminded them.

"Besides, everyone will know about it anyway," Cloe told them. "I mean, our show was the top-rated series of the summer. I bet Miss Berand is the only person in the whole school who didn't know what we did this summer already."

"That might be true," Sasha agreed. "And I

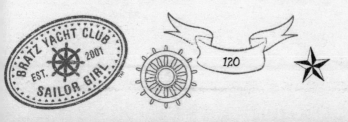

bet she'll become a loyal viewer now!"

"For sure," Yasmin replied. "So, should we go plan out this weekend's trip to Hawaii?"

"Sounds good to me," Sasha declared. "I've made a list of all the beaches I think we should go to, and obviously we should check out a luau, but I'm flexible."

"Oh yeah, when I think 'Sasha', I think 'flexible'," Jade teased.

"Hey, I was pretty flexible on this trip!" Sasha protested. "I didn't make you guys plan a single thing in Greece!"

"It's true, she didn't," Cloe concurred.

"See, that's real improvement," Yasmin added. "Clearly this show is a positive influence in her life!"

"You know who's a positive influence in her life?" Jade asked, grinning. "A certain

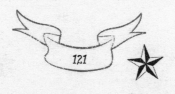

121

fellow traveller who goes by the name of Trevor."

"Oh, I miss those guys!" Cloe cried. "They were so much fun!"

"Cloe, chill," Jade said. "We're seeing them in four days!"

"That's true," Cloe admitted. "I guess that's not such a long time."

"And then we'll be in Maui, enjoying the ocean breezes and fresh pineapple and incredible tropical flowers," Yasmin added.

"Ooh, yeah, I think I miss ocean breezes even more than our co-hosts!" Cloe exclaimed.

"I'm sure the guys would be thrilled to hear that," Jade replied, shaking her head at Cloe.

"I'm just saying, there's nothing like standing at the edge of the ocean with the

wind whipping through your hair and sparkling blue water as far as the eye can see," Cloe explained. "What can compete with that?"

"Not much!" Yasmin agreed.

They all paused in the school hallway, laden down with their book bags and purses, and pictured the ocean that they would be greeting again in just a few short days.

 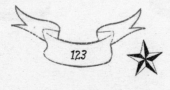 

123

©MGA

Read more about Bratz in these other awesome books!

BRATZ™